Writer's Block Artist's Medley

Story by Fred Marrs

Illustration by Lori Duryea

Mother's House Publishing inc.

Illustrated by Lori Duryea.

Published by
Mother's House Publishing
Distinctive Books of Purity and Purpose
2814 E Woodmen Road
Colorado Springs CO 80920
719-266-0437 / 800-266-0999
info@mothershousepublishing.com
www.mothershousepublishing.com

ISBN 978-1-61888-145-8 hardcover

Tick-tock, tick-tock,
the Writer's got an intellect lock.
He had mustered up the perfect words,
or at least he had promptly thought,
but nothing more than "open winds"
of heaven's vent he had merely brought.
Then swiftly, from around the bend,
and approaching from afar,
came color- full of sassy and over-bold,
wondering what the chances are?
Beginning to splash and dance with paint,
artwork beacon-bright...
shouting out, "A painter's splash doth homage",
to a young child's imaginary sight.
Tick-tack, tick-tack,
the creative's metronome is on-track!

"A Child's Imagination is the
Art of Seeing the Invisible."

Lori Duryea

Tick-tock, tick-tock...

Someone's got writer's block.

I summon words to come forth
like a lion from a cage
a brainstorm of ideas,
from a self-proclaimed sage!

I want to be a writer,

I must prove
one thing true,

I haven't had an idea for weeks, but I know what I must do!

6

I have had ideas before, I'll have them once again,

Where do they come from?
Where do they begin?

To write those ideas, upon the tablet

a constant reminder
I must make it a habit.

I need to keep it fresh,
I need to
keep it new,

The words have escaped me, I know that this is true.

If those same words could talk,
they'd say don't be so coarse.
Fact of the matter, truth be known,
you had forsaken us first.

As the artist stands alone,
in a room with an open door,
seeking a glimpse of an image,
she had never seen before.

Forsaken by the pen from the one who begs, you only need to begin!

At a loss for an image,
at a loss for words
that make it right,
that, in turn, could make
the printed page bright.

With color,
and with purpose,

she could make
images with style,

from the
Author
to the
Artist,
he could
make
the words
worth-while.

She could use some words of encouragement, written down upon the page, that paint a picture perfect, from that self-proclaimed sage.

"Just one idea, I promise"
came the words
from inside the door,

So she sat at her desk
with an easel...
paintbrush in her mouth,
as the author pleaded for more.

...then in her hand, paint at the ready, soon all will be done, it had gone just as she had planned.

23

At this time,
the Artist
felt clever,
as she
shouted out
with a scream,
"Better later
than never!"

24

Story by: Fred Marrs

Fred started writing stories in the '80s.
After writing several quality short-stories, Fred progresed
through college writing about his own personal life experences.
It wasn't too much longer before he quickly gained encouragement
from friends and family to begin writing poetry.
Keeping the heart of a young child's interests,
Fred understood and promised: whether you're
6 or 66, 9 or 99, he will be sure to make you laugh!

Education:
Bachelor of Arts / Secondary Education
Mid-America Bible College 1992-1997
Experience:
Approx. 18-20 years working with students
with various challenges and unique abilities.

Fred Marrs

Illustraton by: Lori Duryea

As a youth, I admired how artists like Norman Rockwell
and Larry Toschik could take a blank piece of paper
and make it come to life with illustration. As I grew
older and began to draw as well, I learned to enjoy
watching each stroke of my own pencil reveal further
enriched features and more enhanced characters
on the page before me. Over time, different aspects
of art have revealed different passageways into
my own imagination.

Education:
Bachelor of Fine Arts / Major: Illustration and Design
Master of Arts / Specialization: K-12 Art Education
Experience:
25 years Advertising, Design, Illustration, Teaching
10 years International / Local Adoption Ministry

ThreeStrands